HOLOCAUST POEMS

and

THOSE OF LIFE CHANGING EVENTS

by

Richard Kalfus

PAGE PUBLISHING, INC.
Conneaut Lake, PA

First originally published by Page Publishing 2021

ISBN 978-1-6624-2418-2 (pbk)
ISBN 978-1-6624-2419-9 (digital)

Printed in the United States of America

CHAPTER 1

About the Poet

Return to Washington Heights

Is it self-indulgence to think
our personal life-stories
have relevance for others?
Are we perhaps only healing ourselves
when we reach into the reservoir
of the past?
Can we speak to others of painful events
with special meaning only for us?

So it is when I reach into my Holocaust past,
marked forever by these events.

Nowhere but in Washington Heights, Manhattan
is this more evident.
Where the largest number of German Jewish
Holocaust
survivors in America live.

I have returned to Washington Heights
to streets of 22 years ago.
I marvel again at the beauty of Fort Tryon Park
overlooking the splendid Hudson River.
I hear German accented English

as in my childhood,
struck by the humor of New York Jews,
mixing Americanisms with German regionalism.
I see 80-year-old Mrs. Dingfelder
born in a Black Forest farm village,
sitting, in a lawn chair
in front of her 6-floor apartment building
quite lost in thought
(memories of the trauma of the past or simply old
age?)

There goes Mr. Marks entering the kosher bakery.
I don't need to go inside to know
what he is ordering:
the family's braided Sabbath Chale

I continue to be touched by Orthodox Mr. Simon
walking to Saturday services,
without money
his apartment keys hanging from his belt.

On Friday services, I stand with others and chant the
Kaddish.
I—for the grandparents
who died at a French Nazi concentration camp.

I—for the Communist uncle shot in the streets of
Karlsruhe by Nazi thugs.
I for the Polish uncle, sister-in-law and their two
young children
murdered in a cattle car on the road to Auschwitz.

I finally *enter* the memory of our old apartment.
a view of the majestic George Washington Bridge,
symbol of the freedom America accorded my parents
and me as their son,
no threat of starvation, isolation, and gas chambers.

I am home…and yet a home never quite released
from memories of Jewish immigrants,
torn from their comfortable Jewish/German lives.

Faced with the challenge:
building new lives
in New York's Washington Heights,
raising a son with only them as a connection
to family lost.

Why I Write Poetry

"So I write poetry," so you say
in a skeptical voice.

It is not foolishness at my age
to face painful feelings
of lost opportunities:
unable once to love more fully
family and friends.

This is the time at
life's last and final stage
to look back with new insight.

Feel the joy, sadness, and regret
of years rushing by to never return.
Once too busy for "just living",
no time for self-reflection.

Now I have the time
I must use it well
"go at it" with the wisdom of old age
taking comfort in the forgiving beauty of poetry.

I am a sage who sees past, present, and future
as a whole to be feared but respected—
an interlocking force in a single life

And I am no longer alone.

Did You Know?

When illness strikes
to control your life.
When pain is a nasty daily visitor
holding you tight
in the grip of old age.

When what remains
are aging memories
of a partner loved
of children young and once dependent
of adults who now need you less
while you yearn to be needed more.

Some turn to faith as a consoling force.
But I have burned those bridges long ago.
For God is no longer a redeeming force.

Yet I have found a way
to console my day
to turn my winter years
into May.
I look to poetry
in its magical world

and find words
which give life to my soul.

While writing I am free
so very briefly
from daily angst
from memories of a past lost.
And I hope again for a new May.
When at my computer
I find the path
once covered with grief
to live now in the present day.

CHAPTER 2

Holocaust Poems and Related Themes

An American Son

"Dad, you gobble up your food
like a vulture eating his prey."
"How can I invite Tommy for supper
when you eat like this?"

I was 13 at the time—a sensitive boy
who knew nothing of what my father
suffered at the hands of the Nazis.

Why was I kept in the dark
about the darkest chapter
in the life of a father I loved?

It was my American mother
who understood him so well.
She knew his fear
in giving voice to the past
and burdening his American son.

So he kept the years of an entire family
lost to himself.

It was years later when I learned
that by protecting me
he was protecting himself
to be able to live in the present
and not in the past.

I have never forgotten the emotional visit to Mrs. Marx; she sits by the window in her Washington Heights apartment. She is the sole survivor of a large family. With a guilt that has no limits, she relives the life of her family before the Holocaust. She sees them as she looks out the window.

She Survived

She survived
on a "Children's Transport"
to England.
But the memory of her mother's
panic attempt
to pull her
from the moving train
has never left her.

And the mother?

As the SS soldier
viciously shoved her
onto a cattle car
bound—she was told—
to the "East,"
she remembered her own
anguish attempt to keep the child
and was grateful
that the daughter would survive.

A Grandson Remembers

She was a small, delicate woman
my grandmother.
She—with only an 8th-grade education
but with the instinct of a survivor.

Raised 3 boys alone
in Nazi Germany.
Deported with thousands of Jews
to Gurs, a French concentration camp.

Max, her eldest
murdered in a Nazi street battle.

Fritz, her youngest,
wife and child
"delivered" to Auschwitz
where none survived.

Allen, my father
by sheer luck
survived in America
where I was born.

A Jewish relief organization
"bought" my grandmother's
freedom to America.

Alas, a new form of survival
was needed
to face a mother-in-law
whose grief at the loss
of her parents, murdered
in the very same camp
as her mother-in-law
knew no bounds.

I too young to recognize
      The emotional abuse
directed at my grandmother
by her mother-in-law,
my mother.

I lived as the silent, powerless son—
a witness in a family
forever marked
by the Holocaust.

Finding Our Humanity

I am a Berliner of a certain age
with a history Germans
want to forget.

My best friend is both a Muslim
and a German.
Together we watch
with compassion
as Syrian refugees
find new hope
in our country.

We take pride
in this challenge,
granting safety
to a terrified people
from a merciless dictator.

Our courage makes us human again—
reminding us of a time
when we Germans forgot
our own humanity.

We The Second Generation

We second generation survivors of the Holocaust
meet once a year remembering November 9, 1938,
when synagogues were torched.
When Jews were forced to leap from their windows.
When neighbors looked on in silence.

Today we can never forget,
the loss and grief
of our Holocaust past.

Each of us has a story to tell:
A mother beaten to death.
A smiling guard overseeing
emaciated Jews as many fall
to their death
in a day and night roll call.

We were seen as mere numbers
in their relentless, murderous task.
a starving Jew, my uncle,
steals food from a dying Jew,
and other frightening Jews look on in despair.

We had a bond, thinking "Oh' how unfair
that we were able to go on living everyday lives,
in the grip of our Holocaust past.

Speak for Them

Dedicated to all docents in every Holocaust museum

Speak for them
As docents
The only way you can
To tell the young and old alike
Of man's inhumanity to man

Of synagogues destroyed
While neighbors silently looked on.

Of an entire kindergarten class
where only one survived.

Of ballet shoes
Without the child

Of eyeglasses piled high
Without faces

Of an only child
Saved on a special train
To families across the sea.

While her parents
On a cattle car train
Transported to Auschwitz.

O' speak to those visitors
With only one thought in mind
That WHAT they now
Have witnessed
Must be passed on to mankind.

Bainbridge Island; Washington

The word spread quickly in our neighborhood.
"I'm sure they are spies," said Mrs. Moore.
So strange—
Their slanted eyes,
Their accented English
They always kept to themselves.

It is easy to see
why they never did fit
in our island neighborhood.

"Hey, wait a minute," protested 15-year-old James.
"That's my school buddy you're talking about
and his English is better than mine."

Fear turned to hatred
in the winter of 1941.
Glad when officials came
with a new law
forcing them out
those alien strangers.

Years later we saw the pictures of German Jews
beaten and dragged from their homes
as neighbors looked on in silence.

My name is James.
But I clearly remember what I was told
Back then in '41.

I am now so ashamed.
I want my grandchildren not to forget
my indifference back then.
So they will never
become what I was.

CHAPTER 3

Poems of Life-Changing Events

A Lament of the Aging

I am old.
So I've been told
By magazines and TV commercials,
Portraying perfect complexions,
Perfect hair, no bald men here.
Perfect, sculpted bodies,
Ready to jog
To save the world
In a cancer run.

I am naked
So many years ago,
Standing before the army doctor
Who wrote, without a word:
"This healthy nineteen-year-old is fit to serve."

A quick glance in the mirror now
Taking note…
The wrinkled, blotchy face
The protruding stomach

The breasts I never had
The bald head of Mr. Clean
Without the muscles
Of a television day.

I look around
In the community pool
At the men and woman of my age
And am comforted
In a grotesque way
To be able to say

I may be one of many
Yet not the worst
Among my peers
In this our final stage.

The Power of Touch

Touching others has profound meaning.
It shows to others that you care
to share another's joy and sadness.

A gay teacher's touch to a troubled child.

A father reaching out to his teenage son,
discovering gay love for the first time.

A homeless man begging money for food,
welcomed both my five-dollar bill
and a silent touch on the shoulder.

An aging parent who, through the years,
loved you for who you are,
now needs your embrace.

Women no longer have the exclusive right
to touch both men and woman.

Men today may hug a friend,
a sign of an enduring bond.

Medical experts all agree:
medication in tandem with a compassionate touch
can effectively help heal
the physical and the emotional pain.

So never forget that by touching,
you receive a gift to yourself.

A young man approached me recently.
I did not recognize him,
but he knew me.
This once homeless man,
now well dressed and smiling
took my hand to thank me:

"You helped me turn my life around."

"Was it my money or my touch?"

The Wife

The two of us, my coworker and I
busy at our computers.

John took out his cell.
"Have to call THE wife, won't take long."
"What? You want to call THE wife?
My surprise meant nothing to him.
At 59, he was very much "old school."
Was he or I the fool?

My young wife had she been there,
she would have told John calmly
that using the word, the, today,
was indeed rare,
and pejorative.

It lowered her to a "possession"—
an object "his" property.

John was baffled, "but, but,
I love my wife…
she is my whole life."

My own wife, having recently
returned from "The Women's March"
could have explained it all.

Would John have understood?

The Changing Face of Barbie

Thank you, Barbie
for looking more like me.
Just one more time.
I am the ugly girl in the mirror
for all to see.
I hear their taunting words:
"You're just too fat."
"Don't you see that?"

Who would imagine that Barbie
would change my fate
in time of late?

Once more I look in my mirror.
Barbie has worked her magic.
I see a different girl so clearly.
Is it merely me?
Bringing into focus a new acceptance
of the real girl to be.

Take note!
You forgot to look beyond
the girl *outside*.

to discover my world *inside.*
A kind and caring girl am I.
One who visits aging Mrs. Foster weekly
in the nursing home.
She and the others marvel at *my beauty*
Loving me for who I am
and my caring sense of duty.

Our Son

We dropped him off, our son
at the state university
just 200 miles from home.
Yet for us, it felt like another country.

Our only son
and we his parents
have lived with *Asperger* most of his 18 years.

Determined to go away to college,
as most everyone in his senior class.

Does this sound like a "setup" by ambitious parents?

It was anything but!

James was good in math and computers,
but no contact to teachers and classmates.

Setting foot on the college campus,
changed our son.

It seemed magical!
He spoke freely to his advisor,

We left James and our heart
on that eventful day in August.

At home, we waited for his first call,
waited to hear about his new roommate,
waited to learn about first day of classes.

Would he "make it"?

Would we?

The Gift of Adoption

As a baby
You came to a new land
To parents who felt blessed
To bring you home.
Your new parents
Knew even before you spoke:
"I am gay"

Here you would be loved,
nurtured and grow
to confront with courage
a new, rich life.

It wasn't easy to find your way.
Growing up, one must say for you
"has always had its ups and downs."

Could this be a sign?
the harder it gets
the greater the joy
as you learn to challenge
those very fears of being gay.

For they lead you
to the person
you are.

The future is bright.
So face every fear.
The good life is near.

Perfection

Was it a blessing or a curse
To have a father
So perfect
As a preacher
And as a father?

In divinity college
As a young pastor
I modeled myself
In his image.

I failed.

I was the imperfect son,
The Asperger son,
The stutterer, the lonely son
Without friends,
The son who took drugs
Who drank too much
To feel less imperfect.

They found him
In a lake.

Was this his way
To perfection?

Friendship

When life seems so unfair
as we age with pain
that lay our very soul so bare.

It us our friends who help us
navigate our fear.
They are near
with compassionate, loving words.

We feel no longer alone.

For this is a gift of friendship
without limits
even to the very end.

The Black and White Cookie

Guilt is
Like a wound that does not heal
Like a broken record
That plays on and on
Like love turned to hate
As my daughter asks:
"What am I?
Black or White?
To Blacks I am White
To Whites I am Black."

For I am the White Mother
Whose one night of sex
Created a child
Who never found a home
With Blacks or Whites

And I must live with
The festering guilt
That it was me
Who created an unhappy child
Who remained an unhappy adult
Blaming me

For bringing her into
A world
Where she remained
Homeless
Forever

Would it be different in July, 2020? For Black lives matter now!

The Elevator

There was a college dean
In a Midwestern city
Who was dressed very well
In a three-piece suit.

Alone in the elevator.
Before the door closed,
A woman appeared.
She saw the man and did not enter.

The man was African American.

Was this Little Rock in 1955?
No, it was 2015
In Ferguson, Missouri

Parenting

Did we know as we had small children
that our worries as parents
would remain ever present in our lives?
Ah, can we do it right!

Grown-up, independent children
remain a part of our inner lives

Oh, how I remember, staying awake to hear
the key in the front door. (our 16-year-old...first-
time driver)

The first prom date. (Do I look lovely/handsome?)

The first ACT scores. (will a scholarship be out there
for me/us?)

The first tearful goodbye at the college dorm.

The first love for dinner with us. (will they like us?)

The first rejection after a job interview. (self-esteemed
tears?)

The first marriage. (hopefully the last…can we afford it?)

The first grandchild. (can the couple juggle job and baby?)

The first time needing advice from our children.

The first time requiring help after surgery.

The first recognition that they were "the adult" and we were
The children.

Ah, for parents, worry is a lifelong job!

CHAPTER 4

Poems of Loss

Cherish Your Loss

With the loss of a love
We feel so alone.
We grope for ways
To escape the pain.

But do not despair
A wise friend once said
"Hold on to those memories
of a past so lovingly lived."

Cherish them!

They are precious gold coins that say:
"Spend us liberally each day
Taking us back to the
joys of the past."

They remain
a gift
a link
To a love that once brightened your life.

So open the lid of those memories
Daily
And ever so slowly
Help lessen the loss and the pain.

LOSS *Dedicated to Pat Scott*

It makes no sense
not in the normal cycle of life
"A child should never in death
precede the parents," they tell me.
"Time will heal," I hear.
"He's in a better place," I hear.
from family
from friends
from colleagues
They sound like nursery rhymes
naïve refrains sung over and over.

I am angry
For I am his mother, his friend,
His protector
"Get out of the sun.
Don't forget your umbrella.
Don't swim where I can't see you."

I even wallow in the thought
of time passing without him.
Is that all that remains?
My anger, my sorrow, my pain?

How can the loss of time together
become less of a loss tomorrow?
How will I ever live again?

A sudden reflex motion
I open my wallet
A photo falls out
In one hand he is holding
A red balloon
In the other hand
his well-used blanket
he is laughing.
I can see that
I can hear that.

And I let go of my anger.
perhaps not forever,
but for now, he is beside me
and I am laughing too.

Memory

Love remains
never lost
though you are gone.

Before me daily
your image never fails
to warm me.

You call me from a business trip.
You check on the children nightly.
You dig in the garden.
You speak long distance
to parents in another city
who nurtured you
before you came to me.

I am forever grateful.

It was a risk you took,
to share a life with me
whom you loved,
but hardly knew.

Yet you knew
long before I did.
So very sure you were.
Sure that:
Different cultures
Different language
Different religion
Were powerless

In the face of love.

Love in the Face of Loss

The pain was real.

She said nothing.

Her sense of taste
was gone forever.

She said nothing.

She googled
information of death.

She said nothing.

Her lovely morning smile
was no longer there

She said nothing.

And then one night
She came to me
in the bed I had taken
when illness

stole from her the joy of touch.

She said nothing.

We made love.

She said nothing.

The silent act of love
said it all!

CHAPTER 5

Humor

I Dream

I am a best-selling author
admired by readers and critics alike.
I am a CEO of a Fortune 500 company
with no visa balance,
with houses in Spain and London.
I throw parties, attracting famous movie stars.
I too am a movie star
who needs a disguise when in public.
I am a government cyber security analyst
who has decoded a terrorist attack.
I am a sought after UN translator.
I have a son
who is an Olympic swimmer,
recently seen on the front page of *Time*.

I am a poet
who has dared to write this nonsense poem!

Humor with a Touch of Nostalgia

Now we are, back once again to Washington Heights.

I am a 73-year-old widower,
In a reflective stage
Joyful memories of my childhood enter my daily routine
While I now live in a world of words
hands frequently on my computer and cell phone
sending out words, in emails and text messages,
to my children living in other houses, in other cities

But words appear inadequate to carry my thoughts.
My past comes alive
when I step out of my cloistered apartment
embracing a world of senses.
Hearing the sounds, inhaling the smells of the past
I capture again my childhood.

The release of the delicious reminder of my mother's stew simmering in the kitchen...
Yes, *I hear* the simmering from my room.
And remember that I must soon finish my math problem

(Oh, I so hated math)
my mother calls out:
"Richie, dinner is ready, wash up."

I was late for dinner that January winter evening,
Shivering in front of the neighborhood pizza place
with high school friends

I can *smell* the fresh snow of the street,
feel the frigid air
h*ear* the snow beneath my feet
trying to avoid, with nose and feet,
the remnants of the neighborhood dogs.
(For this is New York City in the '50s,
not yet "curb your dog" friendly.)

On other evenings, I greet my father at the door
and *smell* his day confined—
to his clothes,
to his very skin,
released from sitting for 8 hours
in his airless office cubicle.
This is the recurring odor of our loving relationship.

I could go on:

The sound of Mrs. Klein's voice as she enters our
apartment:
"Oh sorry, you are still eating?"
And hear my father's German-accented English:
"Come in you beautiful woman."
(I thought she was anything but beautiful.)
Enter neighbor Ruby followed by the aroma of her
menthol cigarette.

Let me end this porthole of selected memory.
As I hear—
the sound of her angry broom
from ceiling below,
announcing, once again,
that our sounds were too much to bear
for her sensitive ears.

Learning to Listen to Others in a Retirement Community

Do remain silent when they tell you their story.

We have children with divorces and new marriages.
(Never cared for the first one!)
We take pride in smart grandchildren.
We had big houses, big bathrooms, big bedrooms
and perhaps a Jacuzzi.
We had good careers with excellent benefits. (Never
needed Obamacare.)
We donate to church charities and cancer research.
We have been eager volunteers at school functions
and half-way houses. (Our names displayed on an
honor roll.)
We donate blood regularly. (Like the juice and
cookie.)
We were good neighbors looking out for one another.
We wrote many Christmas cards. (Even to friends we
have never seen in years.)
We have numerous aches and pains. (Let me tell you
how hard it is mornings to get out of bed?)

We have high cholesterol, have had knee and hip surgery. (You can't tell, can you?)
We have an alarm system for medication reminders. (Shall I tell you how many pills we take each day?)

OK, you've been blissfully quiet:

Now it is your turn!

Dinner at a Retirement Home
(Two Residents at a Table Opposite Ends)

WHAT'S A FOB?

WHAT? YOU'RE STILL WORKING?

NO, I SAID FOB, NOT JOB!

WELL, YOU DON'T HAVE TO RAISE YOUR VOICE
I HEAR PERFECTLY FINE
ME TOO

SO WHAT'S A FOB?
NEVER HAD ONE

AH, YOU'RE NEW HERE, I FEAR
YOU SURE NEED ORIENTATION

I'LL EXPLAIN
IT IS LIKE A KEY
TO OPEN DOORS ALL THE TIME
AND YOU'LL BE FINE
JUST NEED PATIENCE

To learn the ropes

Hey, I am not a patient

I didn't say that

And I am not fat
Work out daily
In the new fitness center

Can you pass the rolls?
I won't eat them

Because you're not fat?

No, doctor's order
But I'd love one

Not my worry

Oh, sorry I got to hurry

Need to see accounting
They added two meals
I never ate them

Me too I'm late
Got all those boxes to unpack

Glad I met you, mate

What? Mate?

Oh, you're not from here?

Lived in Sydney several years

You'll like it here
Just keep your fob always handy
And you'll be just dandy.

Part of a drama club

The Sons-in-Law (phone conversation)

Hi, Lois.
So your son-in-law called you again?
Not my son-in-law: MY ex-son-in-law
How nice that he calls you.
I have another ex-son-in-law
And?
He also calls me often.
Speaks for your nonjudgmental nature.

Wish my only son-in-law were so nice.

Two daughters, two marriages
Two sons-in-laws; two ex-sons-in-law
Interesting family you have.
Yes, and my husband and I—married 40 years now.

Yes, it is a different world.

And that's not all.
I have two biological grandchildren,
And five step-grandchildren.

Expensive isn't it?
Birthdays, Christmas, graduation gifts for all.

Sorry, I hear the doorbell.
Who was that?
Two flower bouquets
Two Mother's Day wishes
two ex-sons-in-law.

Alliteration Can Be Dangerous

If you don't know how to use it.
Lovelorn lovers like the rapids of the river as
they set their sights
on a cove covered with coziness
where they could *hug for hours*
to the beat of their throbbing hearts.

But what will wait for them
If caught
They may be *young yearning*
for long awaited lust
like the last movie stars they saw
ravishing one another in a romp
in the riverbed.

Alas, these *teens try, in vain, to temper*
their desires.

Forgotten for now
those parental rents
from parents to whom
they must answer their

lusting lapse in judgement.

About the Author

Richard Kalfus, PhD from Washington University, St. Louis, Missouri. He is a retired professor, after forty-six years, of Holocaust/Genocide, German/French at St. Louis Community College and St. Louis University. He has received many awards, notably Teacher of the Year from the National Community College Humanities Association.